2 6 NOV 2022

To renew, find us online at:
https://prism.librarymanagementcloud.co.uk/bromley
Please note: Items from the adult library may also
accrue overdue charges when borrowed on
children's tickets.

In partnership with

Usborne Bug Tales

The Fly who told a Lie

Russell Punter

Illustrated by Siân Roberts

In this story,
you'll meet Bee,

plus Slug...

and Dragonfly.

There's Beetle,

hornets,

lots of ants...

and the fly
who told a lie.

Bee is making honey buns, when...

CRASH! THUD!

What was that?

She buzzes off to see
what's wrong.

A ball lies on her mat.

Beside it lies some
broken glass.

"My window's smashed.
Oh no."

She soon spies Guy the fly
outside.

"I didn't do it,"
Guy replies.

"Hmm, are you sure?"
asks Bee.

"I saw what happened,"
Guy explains.

"I'm not to blame,
you'll see..."

"It all began with Slug..." says Guy,

"I saw him by the lake.

Then Dragonfly swooped
down on him...

and took his creamy cake.

Dragonfly whizzed off
so fast...

she zoomed right
into Toad.

12

The cake went flying from her grasp...

and landed on the road.

Just then, Beetle
jogged along.

She slipped on all
the cream.

Her little legs just
couldn't grip.

"Please help!" I heard
her scream.

She swerved and tumbled
down a hill.

It really was
quite steep.

She slid, slap bang,
against a tree...

and lay there in a heap.

Beetle staggered
to her feet.

But she'd no time to rest.

Her noisy crash
against the tree
had smashed a
hornets' nest.

The angry hornets
buzzed around.

"Our home is wrecked,"
they said.

The hornets went into a dive.

So Beetle quickly fled.

Speedy Beetle ran
and ran,

the hornets on her heels.

She spotted Maggot's tractor parked...

and leaped behind the wheel.

She drove along the
road, but then...

"I can't stop!" came
her cry.

She crashed into
a five-bar gate...

CRUNCH!

and through the
field nearby.

25

This was the local soccer field.

A game was underway.

"Are you crazy?" cried
the ants.

"Keep off, or we
can't play!"

"Stop that tractor!"
begged the ants.

"But I *can't* stop it!"
Beetle yelled.

The ants ran for
their lives.

Beetle jumped out
of the cab.

The tractor kept
on going.

30

"Will nothing stop it?"
someone asked.

We had no way
of knowing.

The tractor sped
out of control.

It scared me. I'm not lying.

It crashed into a
storage shed...

and twenty balls
went flying.

One ball landed
near your house...

and bounced upon
the grass.

It whizzed towards
your window pane...

and smashed right
through the glass.

So that's the story,"
Guy declares.

"I swear each word is true."

"That's quite a tale you told," says Bee.

Does this belong to you?

"You don't believe my tale?" says Guy.

Bee reads the writing on the ball...

"Oh, er, well then..."
mumbles Guy.

"I'm sure I can explain..."

"Now, no more lies please, Guy," says Bee.

She taps her window pane.

"Please pay to get it fixed,"
says Bee.

"I have no cash!"
wails Guy.

"Then do some jobs for
me instead."

Guy nods and gives a sigh.

Guy works hard
from dawn to dusk.

He sweeps inside and out.

He cleans Bee's car,

and mows her lawn,

until he's tired out.

"I really have,"
says Guy.

"I'll tell the truth
from this day on.

Believe me, that's no lie!"

Series editor: Lesley Sims
Designed by Laura Bridges

Reading consultant: Alison Kelly

First published in 2022 by Usborne Publishing Ltd., Usborne House,
83-85 Saffron Hill, London EC1N 8RT, England. usborne.com
Copyright © 2022 Usborne Publishing Ltd.